PROJECT BRIGHT SPARK

Written by Annabel Pitcher

Illustrated by Roger Simó

Collins

CHAPTER 1

It may not have been on the TV news channels or even in the national newspapers, but when my favourite teacher, Miss Cartwright, was fired by the Head, it was one of the biggest scandals there'd ever been in the village of Much Marcle. And it would've been the biggest if it hadn't been for all that stuff to do with Mr Crabtree a year ago.

Mr Crabtree lived in Coldwood Manor, a huge house at the top of the highest hill in my village. Dressed in expensive clothes, with slicked-back dark hair and greedy blue eyes, Mr Crabtree spent his time in his mansion counting his money and concocting cruel plans to get even more wealth and power. Twelve months ago, he came up with his cruellest plan yet, inventing a machine to listen in to people's phone calls, finding out their secrets and using them as blackmail.

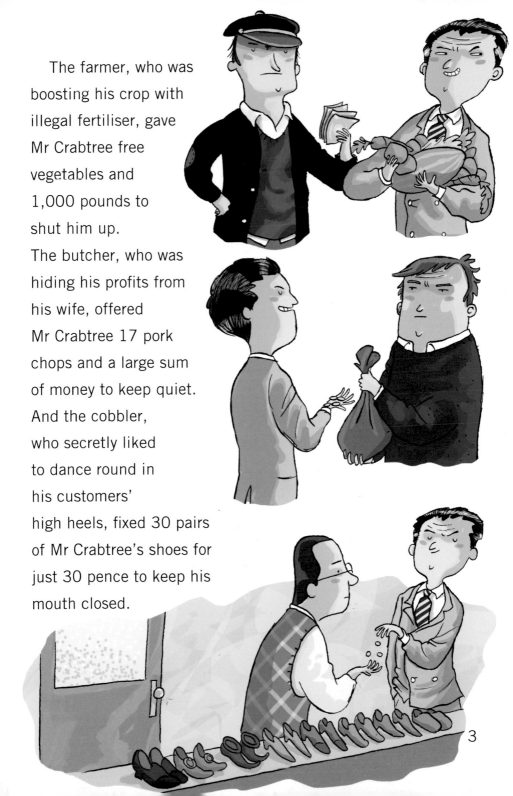

The farmer, who was boosting his crop with illegal fertiliser, gave Mr Crabtree free vegetables and 1,000 pounds to shut him up.

The butcher, who was hiding his profits from his wife, offered Mr Crabtree 17 pork chops and a large sum of money to keep quiet.

And the cobbler, who secretly liked to dance round in his customers' high heels, fixed 30 pairs of Mr Crabtree's shoes for just 30 pence to keep his mouth closed.

3

It wasn't until Mr Crabtree tried to blackmail old Wanda Watson that he got caught out. Totally unafraid, she hobbled down to the police station in broad daylight in pink slippers and a frilly dressing gown to tell PC Pritchard what was going on.

"I'm not embarrassed to admit that I wear my pyjamas all day, eat cereal straight out of the box and watch five hours of quiz shows back-to-back with my poodles!" she cried. "I'm 77 years old. I can do what I like. That crook can't shame *me* into giving him my savings!"

Mr Crabtree was arrested but, as everyone else in Much Marcle was too afraid to give evidence, he got away with his crime and returned to Coldwood Manor in his bright yellow sports car, his blue eyes gleaming in triumph.

So that was the biggest scandal in my village, but the one concerning Miss Cartwright was almost as huge, and no one talked about anything else during the Christmas holidays. You see, Miss Cartwright was just about the nicest person you could ever meet, so it was a big shock when the Head announced she'd stolen money that was meant for our school trip to London. Of course, I told everybody that she couldn't possibly have done it, but that's the problem with adults: sometimes they can't see things that are really obvious to us kids.

I knew straight away that I wasn't going to like her replacement, Mr Spark. The feeling was mutual. He seemed to hate everyone in the class – well, everyone except Mildred, Mr Crabtree's daughter.

"Briony Davies," said Mr Spark, "if I want you to answer the question, I'll tell you to put up your hand. Now shut up and listen to Mildred."

"The capital city of France is Moscow," said Mildred, with a spitefully smug look in my direction. She'd inherited her father's dark hair and blue eyes, but none of his brains. Not that Mr Spark seemed to have noticed.

"Excellent! Correct again, Mildred," he said. "Your fifteenth gold star."

Nobody else in the class had a single star and, by this point, my best friend Sergio had clearly had enough.

"But that's wrong!" he cried, his hands in his brown curls. "The capital of France isn't Moscow – it's Paris. Are you saying that the Eiffel Tower, one of the most famous *French* monuments in the world, is actually in *Moscow*?"

Mr Spark swivelled to look at him with lifeless black eyes. "No, you silly boy! The Eiffel Tower is in Paris in France. Now, be quiet."

Sergio shook his head in disbelief and I nodded to show that I understood.

"There's something strange about that Mr Spark,"
he said finally, as we walked through the school gates
at the end of the day. "Today we've learnt that
11 x 8 is 19, a full stop is used when you can't be
bothered to write any more, and Washington DC
is not the capital of the USA but the name of
a type of washing machine. It's ridiculous!
I mean, I'd expect those answers from Mildred, but why
doesn't Mr Spark correct her? And why won't he give
anyone else a chance to answer a question?"

I was just about to answer when a bright yellow
sports car swerved through the school gates at high speed.
Leaping out of the way, I turned around angrily.
The driver went sailing past the visitors' car park and
swung into the section marked *"DISABLED BADGE
HOLDERS ONLY"*. A thin man with slicked-back dark
hair climbed out from the driver's seat as Mildred
showed off the gold sticker that Mr Spark had presented
her for saying Henry VIII had beheaded 19 wives,
12 of whom were called Briony. The same spiteful,
smug smile that Mildred had given me spread across
Mr Crabtree's pointed face.

"They're up to something," I muttered with a frown.

"Yeah," Sergio whispered. "But what?"

9

CHAPTER 2

I tried to tell my parents that something strange was going on, but no matter how much I complained, they just wouldn't listen.

"But we're not learning *anything*! And Mr Spark rewards Mildred for *everything*. It's so weird!"

"Are you sure you're not jealous, love?" asked Dad, cutting a sausage in half as we ate at the kitchen table. "I know you're used to being top of the class, but perhaps you're taking it a little too easy. You need to try harder to impress Mr Spark. I did always wonder if Miss Cartwright was a little soft, you know. Mildred is obviously doing something right."

"If by *doing something right* you mean *getting everything wrong*, then yes she is!"

"Now that's enough," replied Dad, thrusting the sausage in my direction. "Perhaps you need some extra lessons to catch up with Mildred. Maybe I should come into school to speak to Mr Spark."

I gave up complaining to adults and hoped school would improve, but the following week things took a turn for the worse.

Mr Spark was in the middle of listing every single river in England and their exact length down to the last centimetre when he stopped suddenly in the middle of his sentence. The class froze. A freckly girl clapped her hands to try and get his attention, but Mr Spark just stood by the whiteboard, completely still, staring into space.

And that's when we heard it for the first time – a strange, metallic whirring sound. Everyone in the class looked around the room for the source of the noise. What on earth was it? And why wasn't Mr Spark moving? Was this some kind of odd test?

Eventually, Mildred piped up: "Excuse me, Mr Spark, is everything OK? Would you like me to answer another question?"

This seemed to do the trick as the whirring noise stopped and Mr Spark jolted back into life, continuing his sentence exactly where he'd left off a minute before.

Mildred was outraged. Mr Spark *never* ignored her! She forced a smile on to her thin lips and tried again: "Excuse me, Mr Spark. I don't think you heard me. I asked if everything was OK and if you'd like me to answer a question."

Mr Spark's reply took everyone by surprise. Without moving his body at all, his head turned and he fixed his blank stare on Mildred. In his coldest voice, he spat: "Briony Davies, you will not speak in my classroom unless I ask you to speak."

I leapt out of my skin. I hadn't said a word! But Mr Spark was still gazing at Mildred, whose mouth had fallen open, making her look like a rather nasty goldfish.

"But ... but ... I'm *Mildred*, Mr Spark, not Briony Davies.
Mildred Crabtree."

"Briony Davies, if I have to tell you to be quiet again,
you will tidy up this entire classroom."

Mildred went bright red. Sergio caught my eye and
I shrugged, totally confused. Deciding to investigate
further, I tightened up my face, stuck my nose
in the air and, without even bothering to put up
my hand, did the best Mildred impression
I could muster. "Excuse me, Mr Spark.
As I'm your very favourite student,
I just wanted to let you know that
eating spinach can turn your
skin green, wearing glasses
gives you x-ray vision
and all the ties in
the world are
made in Thailand."

Quick as a flash, Mr Spark's head swivelled in my direction. Sergio winced, his hands covering his face, waiting for the explosion.

"Excellent. Correct again, Mildred. Three gold stars!"

Now it was my turn to look like a goldfish. Mr Spark stuck the stars next to Mildred's name and went back to telling us about the rivers of England as we all sat there in stunned silence.

CHAPTER 3

"I didn't know you could do such a good Mildred impression," chuckled Sergio. "You should've seen her face! She couldn't complain either because you'd just earned her a load more stars!"

He shot the basketball through the net for the third time in a row. As the final bell had rung that afternoon, we'd agreed that it was time to investigate Mr Spark and had decided to meet back at the school playground to make a plan.

"But why did he just stand there saying nothing for a whole minute?" I asked. "And what was that whirring noise in the classroom?"

"I dunno," said Sergio.

"And we still haven't worked out why he's so desperate for Mildred to be top of the class!"

"It's Mildred," replied Sergio.

"Well obviously, but what is it about her?"

"*No.* Over there!" Sergio said, pointing over my shoulder in the direction of the school. "*It's Mildred and her dad!*"

I spun round and, sure enough, Mr Crabtree and his daughter were climbing out of the yellow sports car, looking around suspiciously.

"Quick! *Hide!*" I whispered.

Sergio didn't need telling twice. We dived behind
a wooden bench.

"Ouch! You're squashing my head," he complained.

"Well, keep it down then or they'll see it poking over
the top!"

"It's not my fault. I've grown ten centimetres since ..."

"... and be quiet!" I interrupted.

After a moment or two, we nodded to each other and peeped
round the end of the bench. We were just in time to see
Mr Crabtree disappear through the front door of the school.

"Let's go!" I said, jumping to my feet.

"Yeah, you're right, we'd better be getting home," said Sergio, checking his watch. "Mum doesn't like me being out after dark."

"Are you kidding?! I mean, *let's go* to the school and have a look! I want to find out what Mildred and Daddy are up to. What are they doing here at this time?"

As if to answer my question, a light suddenly went on in the school building.

"Isn't that our classroom?" asked Sergio.

Fear and excitement buzzed through me as we crept across the playground and up the grass bank to the car park. Sprinting across the tarmac, we flattened ourselves against the wall of the school, breathing hard. We ducked down beneath the level of the classroom window.

Slowly, slowly we lifted up our heads. A row of folders on the windowsill meant that we didn't have a full view of the room. Mildred and Mr Crabtree were standing in front of the teacher's desk with their backs to us, talking quickly. We leant in, pressing our ears to the glass, desperate to hear what they were saying.

"But you promised, Daddy. You *promised*. You said that if we could get rid of that annoying Miss Cartwright, you'd make sure I'd be top of the class. It was so embarrassing today. You must fix it!"

"Hasn't everything worked perfectly so far?" Mr Crabtree said in an oily, sneering voice. "Don't you have a new teacher? Aren't you receiving more gold stars than anyone in the class? Mr Spark has done everything that you wanted him to do, even teaching that annoying Briony Davies girl a lesson. He can't be perfect all the time."

Sergio stared at me, the same horrified look on his face that I must have had on mine. We'd known Mr Spark was being unfair, but we'd never imagined it was because he was actually working *for* Mr Crabtree. And poor Miss Cartwright! I knew she couldn't have stolen that money!

I turned back to the window and, just as I was wondering why Mildred and her dad had risked breaking into the school to have this conversation when they could easily have had it at home, it all became clear. Raising my head to get a better view over the folders, Mr Crabtree stepped away from the teacher's desk – and there, sitting bolt upright in the teacher's chair, was Mr Spark.

My hand flew to my mouth. He wasn't looking at Mildred, nor was he looking at Mr Crabtree; he was staring straight ahead, past the row of folders against the window. Straight at me.

CHAPTER 4

Hearts pounding, we sprinted across the pitch-black school fields, wriggling under the gap in the hedge and dashing as fast as we could along the road. Sergio puffed along behind me, trying to keep up. As I finally slowed down, he grabbed

the back of my t-shirt, pulling me to a stop outside his house.

"What ... was ... all ... that ... about?" he forced out, clutching his sides.

I just had time to explain that I'd seen Mr Spark in the classroom and that he'd spotted me peering

through the window before Sergio's mum opened the front door, her hands on her hips and her face furious.

"I'd better go," Sergio muttered, going pale. "See you tomorrow."

Tomorrow. I was dreading it, and I tossed and turned all night, imagining what punishment Mr Spark would give me for snooping.

At school, yawning and puffy-eyed, I tried to sneak over to my seat without being noticed. As Mr Spark went through the register, I didn't dare look up. I felt sure he'd say something. But he didn't. The day started as normally as it ever did with Mr Spark as the teacher. Neither he nor Mildred said a word to me.

"Well, they might want to pretend the secret meeting in the classroom didn't happen, but I'm not about to forget it," I said to Sergio at break. "And poor Miss Cartwright! We need some kind of proof so we can clear her name!"

Determined to save our old teacher, we set about trying to catch Mildred and Mr Spark in secret conversations. I tried to listen in when Mildred was speaking to her dad at the end of school, and a few days later I even pretended to be Mildred again, but Mr Spark seemed to have remembered who I was and just made me clean out the art cupboard.

"Well, the last impression you did was much better," said Sergio, trying not to laugh as I appeared at the end of lunch with paint all over my hands. "This one probably deserved a detention."

I didn't find it funny. I was getting so frustrated. I didn't giggle with everyone else when Mr Spark forgot to sit down after the hymn in assembly. I didn't laugh when he repeated Sergio's name 18 times when he was doing the register one morning. And I didn't even raise a smile when he taught a whole numeracy lesson facing in the wrong direction, and a whole literacy lesson reading a book upside down.

"I'll get to the bottom of it soon," I promised myself, clenching my fists. "I just need a chance to get closer to the Crabtrees."

That came sooner than expected when Mildred stood up in front of the whole class the following week during silent reading. She cleared her throat importantly.

"I have a special announcement," she declared. "This Sunday is my birthday."

Paul Pritchard leapt to his feet and, eyeing up Mr Spark and the star chart, started to applaud. "Three cheers for Mildred's birthday. Well done, Mildred!"

Mildred glared and cut across him. "Don't interrupt me. That's not the announcement!"

Paul sat down looking a little disappointed.

Mildred continued sharply. "*As I was saying*, this Sunday is my birthday, and to celebrate you're all invited to a party at my house, Coldwood Manor."

"*All* of us?" I asked before I could stop myself. I couldn't hide the surprise in my voice.

"Yes, Briony. *Even* you and Sergio."

"As if we'd go!" Sergio sniggered behind his book. "She only wants to show off the size of her mansion."

"I'm going," I whispered.

"But I thought you hated Mildred! Honestly, why do girls change their minds so much?"

"And why do boys need everything explaining to them?" I replied in a low voice. "I'm not going to the party for *fun*. I'm going to investigate. And so are you!"

Sergio's eyebrows crumpled. "I don't know. I'm still in trouble for the last time we *investigated* this, and my mum said –"

"We'd love to come to your party," I interrupted him loudly, beaming at Mildred. She nodded without smiling as Sergio's chin slumped on to his hand.

CHAPTER 5

"This is the worst party I've ever been to," Sergio whispered in the posh dining room of Coldwood Manor. The whole class was sitting round the edge of the large room on hard-backed chairs as Mildred opened her last present and tossed it ungratefully to one side.

"We're here to solve a mystery. We're not supposed to be having the time of our lives," I hissed.

"Good job really," Sergio replied, as Mildred lined up her presents in size order so she could decide on her favourite. Dressed in a pale blue dress, long white socks and black buckled shoes, she marched up and down the row, tapping her chin with her finger.

At that precise moment, a strange whirring noise drifted into the room. I sat up straighter. It was coming from upstairs – the same whirring noise I'd heard at school! It stopped abruptly, started once more, and then died completely. I nudged Sergio, who nodded to say he'd heard it too. We needed to find an excuse to leave the dining room, and fast.

"And the prize for best gift goes to ... *Paul Pritchard!*" Mildred announced in a shrill voice as though she was handing out awards at the Oscars.

Paul Pritchard leapt up from his chair by the door, overcome by his success. "Three cheers for Mildred!" he cried, throwing his arms above his head just as a servant walked into the dining room.

Before anyone could shout "*Hip hip hooray*",
Paul Pritchard's flailing hand connected with the huge tray
of food that the servant was carrying. It spun into the air.
Sausage rolls, cakes, crisps, biscuits and all other manner
of party food flew in all directions and a particularly
creamy-looking cupcake landed with a splat on Mildred's dress.

Everyone in the room seemed to hold their breath.
Mildred glared at the servant whose hand was still holding
an imaginary tray. She glared at Paul Pritchard who was
still standing with his arms above his head as if he didn't
dare move. Finally, Mildred glared at the cupcake, which,
as if on cue, plopped on to the floor leaving a big gooey
white ring on her clean blue dress.

And then came the tantrum. She screamed, she shouted,
she kicked the presents, she kicked the food on the floor
and she even kicked Paul Pritchard. Mildred stormed out of
the room shouting for her father, causing such a racket that she
gave us exactly the opportunity we'd been waiting for.

"Now!" I said to Sergio. "Let's go!"

Having narrowly avoided being hit by a flying pork pie, he jumped to his feet, looking relieved. We sprinted to the door and peered out into the hall. Voices were coming from upstairs.

"I thought I told you not to disturb me whilst I'm working!" growled Mr Crabtree.

"But that stupid boy has ruined my party, Daddy. I want him to leave. You have to send him away! And order the servants to make more food. I'll scream until you do!"

Thankfully, Mr Crabtree could see his daughter was in no mood to be refused. Instead, he muttered something angrily and started down the stairs. Hearts racing, Sergio and I ran across the hall and crouched behind a coat-stand as Mr Crabtree marched into the dining room.

"What now?" Sergio asked in a tense whisper after we'd ducked out from our hiding place and dashed up to the first floor without being seen.

"Let's start in there!" I said, pointing to a room that had a light shining through the open door. "It looks like his study. If Mr Crabtree is up to something, I bet we'll find a clue in there!"

As Paul Pritchard howled below, we glanced over our shoulders to check the coast was clear, and then slipped inside.

CHAPTER 6

I scanned the room quickly. It was large and dark with wooden panels on the wall that were mostly hidden by high bookshelves. In the far corner, there was a huge oak cupboard. The only other furniture in the study was a brown leather sofa and a solid wooden desk with a chair behind it, a pile of papers spread out on top.

We tore to the desk and started to flick through the documents at top speed. We knew we couldn't have long before Mr Crabtree came back.

"What are those?" I breathed, as Sergio picked up two pieces of paper.

"They look like designs for some sort of invention," he said, pointing to the detailed images. The first looked like a picture of a policeman underneath the name Robert "Bobby" Copperfield, and the second looked like a diagram of a bank worker, labelled William "Bill" Teller. "What do you reckon they are?"

"No idea! But they're nothing to do with Mr Spark, so let's keep searching! There must be something ..."

"What's that noise?" Sergio interrupted, his face draining of colour.

"Footsteps!"

"We've got to get out of here! *Now!*"

"Not yet!" I muttered, my frustration boiling up. "I'm not leaving without proof. I know there's something about Mr Spark in here!"

The footsteps were almost at the top of the stairs now.

"I'll buy you some time!" Sergio hissed, dashing out of the study door without a moment to spare.

"What are you doing up here, boy?" Mr Crabtree asked as I rifled through the papers with trembling hands. "I thought my daughter made it perfectly clear when you arrived that nobody was to leave the dining room."

"I ... I was looking for the bathroom. I was desperate. You know how it is, Mr Crabtree. I couldn't wait. And I didn't want to make a big song and dance of it in front of everybody so ..."

"Get back downstairs," Mr Crabtree ordered.

"But –"

"*GO!*"

My stomach clenched horribly. There was nothing whatsoever on the desk about Mr Spark and now I was trapped inside the study! I heard Sergio run down the stairs as I darted to the oak cupboard to hide, but just as I was about to grab the handle, something caught my interest. On the other side of the room, tucked almost out of sight on the end of one of the bookshelves, was a thin blue folder with three words written in black letters on the front: PROJECT BRIGHT SPARK.

CHAPTER 7

I held my breath, lowering my eye to the keyhole. I'd only just made it to the cupboard in time. Mr Crabtree was back at his desk and, by the way he was working, obviously hadn't noticed anything suspicious. Carefully, I opened the thin blue folder and held it up to the light of the keyhole.

My eyes widened as I discovered how Mildred had stolen the school trip money, putting it in Miss Cartwright's purse to get her sacked. My mouth dropped as I learnt how Mr Crabtree had called up the school, pretending to be a headteacher himself, saying that Mr Spark came "Highly recommended". My insides twisted as I read about Mr Spark's instructions to put Mildred to the top of the class. And my skin went cold as I saw that next to my own name were the sinister words: *teach her a lesson*.

Only one page confused me – a labelled diagram of Mr Spark, similar to the picture of the policeman and the bank worker on Mr Crabtree's desk. Frowning, I studied the page more closely. There was lots of technical stuff that didn't make any sense because it talked about wires and batteries and electrical parts. Had Mr Spark been an electrician in the past? Given how bad he was at teaching, that might make sense.

The time dragged on. A clock ticked slowly. Mr Crabtree's pen scratched across a piece of paper.

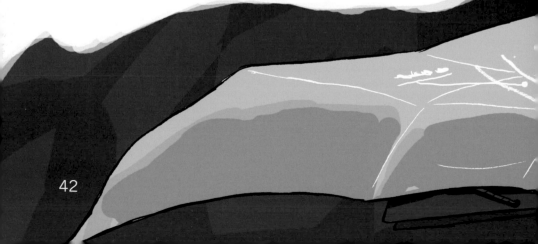

I was beginning to wonder how I was ever going to get out of the cupboard. I thought I could hear the other children putting on their coats downstairs as if the party had finished. What if Mr Crabtree didn't leave the room all night? My parents would be so worried!

I sat down, anxious, resting my head against the wood, and realised for the first time that the cupboard was a lot deeper than I'd imagined. What I'd thought was the back was really just a thick, black curtain. What was that doing there? Mouth dry, I moved it gently to one side and peered into a secret compartment. A large, dark shape loomed in the shadows. A prickle of fear that I couldn't quite explain started to creep up my spine. Scrambling silently to my knees, I leant forward, screwing up my eyes: a white shirt ... a grey tie ... a cold, unsmiling face ...

Mr Spark!

I forced my hand over my mouth in an effort not to scream, but I couldn't stop myself from stumbling. I bumped into Mr Spark and he seemed to rock in slow motion – once, twice, three times – and then he toppled over with a metallic sort of crash as a screw fell out of a joint in his neck and I finally understood what was going on. The lifeless eyes ... The swivelling neck ... The weird behaviour that didn't seem human ... It's because it *wasn't* human! Mr Spark was an invention! A robot made by Mr Crabtree and programmed to put Mildred to the top of the class! And by the look of the other designs on the desk, Mr Spark wasn't the only robot in Much Marcle. There was one in the police station and another in the bank!

A chair scraped on the wooden floor in the study, as if it had been pushed back.

"What's going on in there?" Mr Crabtree roared, flinging open the cupboard door.

He gasped when he saw me crouching in the corner, and thrust out a hand as if to grab my arm, but a loud bang made him stop short. Mr Spark was climbing to his feet, the whirring that I'd heard in the classroom coming right from his chest! And not just that – Mr Spark's body was fizzing and crackling too.

Taking advantage of Mr Crabtree's hesitation, I ducked under his arm. I was across the room in three strides and just about to escape into the hall when I heard an odd shout. Mr Spark was gripping Mr Crabtree by the shoulder.

"Briony Davies, I must teach you a lesson," said Mr Spark.

"But I'm not Briony Davies. I'm Gregory Crabtree. You must follow my instructions!"

"Be quiet, Briony Davies! You will speak when I ask you to speak. I must teach you a lesson."

I couldn't help myself. I turned round to see Mr Spark
throwing Mr Crabtree over his shoulder and into the cupboard.
There was a thump and then nothing. Mr Spark slammed
the door behind him. His head swivelled right the way round
twice before his eyes came to rest on me.

I didn't wait to hear Mr Spark repeat his favourite phrase. Yanking the door shut behind me, I turned right, sprinting down a corridor with my blood thumping in my ears. I skidded to a halt, letting out a cry of fear. It was a dead end! There was nothing but a big glass window in front of me. I spun round to run back the way I'd come, but it was too late. Mr Spark was already standing there, blocking my way. Sparks popped from his neck and his eyes glowed red.

Jerkily, he started to move towards me, getting faster and faster, nearer and nearer. I did the only thing that came into my mind. Tightening up my face, I stuck my nose in the air.

"Excuse me, Mr Spark. I'm Mildred Crabtree, your favourite student."

He stopped suddenly, confused. His head sparked like his hair was on fire. Hopping on the spot, he counted backwards from 20 at top speed and listed the rivers in England in size order. And then, with one final hissing bend of the knees, Mr Spark launched himself into the air and went crashing through the big glass window. Before he fell, I could just make out his final words:
"Three gold stars for you, Mildred!"

There was a mighty smash down below. When I looked out through the hole in the window, I could see one very damaged yellow sports car with a Mr Spark-shaped hole in the roof. Wires and screws littered the ground in front of my shocked classmates and their parents, as a lady in pink slippers and a frilly dressing gown held up a broken piece of steaming metal that used to be Mr Spark's face. PC Pritchard, Paul's dad, ran towards the house and came back seconds later with Mr Crabtree in handcuffs.

"I told you he was a crook!" said old Wanda Watson, there to collect her granddaughter. "Now let's get that lovely Miss Cartwright back to teach you kids!"

As all the children cheered, Sergio looked up at me through the broken window with a huge grin on his face and his thumbs held up high. And I have to admit, I agreed with him when he said to me on the way home, "That must have been your best Mildred impression yet!"

Clue 1:

Our new teacher, Mr Spark, hates everyone in the class – except for Mildred Crabtree.

Clue 2:

There's a metallic whirring noise in our classroom.

Clue 3:

Mr Spark behaves strangely – he even muddles up me and Mildred.

Clue 4:

Mr Crabtree and Mildred have a secret meeting with Mr Spark.

Clue 5:

Mr Crabtree says he got rid of Miss Cartwright.

54

57 35

Clue 6:

Mr Spark is working for

Mr Crabtree.

Clue 7:

There's a folder called

Project Bright Spark in

Mr Crabtree's study.

Clue 8:

There's also a labelled

electrical diagram of

Mr Spark.

Clue 9:

Mr Spark is hidden in

Mr Crabtree's study.

Clue 10:

Mr Spark is a robot!

55

FAKE
BEARD

Ideas for reading

Written by Linda Pagett B.Ed (hons), M.Ed
Lecturer and Educational Consultant

Learning objectives: sustain engagement with longer texts, using different techniques to make the text come alive; use a range of oral techniques to present persuasive arguments; improvise using a range of drama strategies and conventions to explore themes such as hopes, fears and desires; devise a performance considering how to adapt for a specific audience

Curriculum links: Citizenship: Choices

Interest words: scandal, slicked-back, blackmail, triumph, smug, outraged, whirring, sneering, snooping, opportunity, tense, impression

Resources: paper and pens

Getting started

This book can be read over two or more reading sessions.

- Ask one child to read the blurb aloud to others and predict what the book will be about from the front cover.

- Demonstrate reading pp2–3 and begin a character sketch of Mr Crabtree. Encourage children to use vocabulary outside the text, e.g. devious, sly, underhand. Investigate clues as to what the author thinks of Crabtree.

Reading and responding

- Encourage children to read up to p10 and then predict what might happen in the story. Make a quick note of these suggestions and add to Crabtree's character sketch, noting how the writer influences our sympathy of the characters, e.g. Coldwood Manor sounds uninviting.

- Stop at p23 and review children's predictions of what would happen in the story. Introduce the word *conspiracy* and discuss who is conspiring and for what.

- Direct children to continue reading quietly to the end of book prompting and praising where necessary. Support them in writing notes of clues they think may be useful for solving the mystery.